Thomas the Tank Engine & Friends

A BRITT ALLCROFT COMPANY PRODUCTION

Based on The Railway Series by The Rev W Awdry
© Gullane (Thomas) LLC 2002

Visit the Thomas & Friends web site at www.thomasthetankengine.com

ISBN 0-439-33849-2

12 11 10 9 8 7 6 5 4 3 2 1   2 3 4 5 6 7/0
Printed in the U.S.A.
First Scholastic printing, May 2002

This edition is available for distribution only through the direct-to-home market.

Trouble in the shed

by
The REV. W. AWDRY

SCHOLASTIC INC.

New York   Toronto   London   Auckland   Sydney
Mexico City   New Delhi   Hong Kong   Buenos Aires

Sir Topham Hatt sat in his office and listened. Sir Topham Hatt frowned and said, "What a nuisance passengers are! How can I work with all this noise?"

The Station-Master knocked and came in, looking worried.

"There's trouble in the shed, Sir. Henry is sulking; there is no train, and the passengers are saying this is a Bad Railway."

"Indeed!" said Sir Topham Hatt. "We cannot allow that. Will you quiet down the passengers, please; I will go and speak to Henry."

He found Henry, Gordon and James looking sulky.

"Come along, Henry," he said, "it is time your train was ready."

"Henry's not going," said Gordon rudely. "We *won't* shunt like Common Tank Engines. We are Important Tender Engines. You fetch our coaches and we will pull them. Tender Engine's don't shunt," and all three engines let off steam in a cheeky way.

"Oh, indeed," said Sir Topham Hatt severely. "We'll see about that; engines on My Railway do as they are told."

He hurried away, climbed into his car and drove to find Edward.

"The yard has never been the same since Thomas left," he thought sadly.

Edward was shunting.

"Leave those freight cars please, Edward; I want you to push coaches for me in the yard."

"Thank you, Sir, that will be a nice change."

"That's a good engine," said Sir Topham Hatt kindly, "off you go then."

So Edward found coaches for the three engines, and that day the trains ran as usual.

But when Sir Topham Hatt came the next morning, Edward looked unhappy.

Gordon came clanking past, hissing rudely. "Bless me!" said Sir Topham Hatt. "What a noise!"

"They all hiss me, Sir," answered Edward sadly. "They say 'Tender Engines don't shunt,' and last night they said I had black wheels. I haven't, have I, Sir?"

"No, Edward, you have nice blue ones, and I'm proud of you. Tender Engines do shunt, but all the same you'd be happier in your own yard. We need a Tank Engine here."

He went to the Engine Workshop, and they showed him all sorts of Tank Engines. There were big ones, and little ones; some looked happy, and some sad, and some looked at him anxiously, hoping he would choose them.

At last he saw a smart little green engine with four wheels.

"That's the one," he thought.

"If I choose you, will you work hard?"

"Oh, Sir! Yes, Sir!"

"That's a good engine; I'll call you Percy."

"Yes, Sir! Thank you, Sir!" said Percy happily.

So he bought Percy and drove him back to the yard.

"Edward," he called, "here's Percy; will you show him everything?"

Percy soon learned what he had to do, and they had a happy afternoon.

Once Henry came by hissing as usual.

"*Whee—eesh!*" said Percy suddenly; Henry jumped and ran back to the shed.

"How beautifully you wheeshed him," laughed Edward. "I can't wheesh like that."

"Oh!" said Percy modestly, "that's nothing; you should hear them in the Workshop. You have to wheesh loudly to make yourself heard."

Next morning Thomas arrived. "Sir Topham Hatt sent for me; I expect he wants help," he said importantly to Edward.

"Sh! Sh! Here he comes."

"Well done, Thomas; you've been quick. Listen, Henry, Gordon and James are sulking; they say they won't shunt like Common Tank Engines. So I have shut them up, and I want you both to run the line."

"Common Tank Engines indeed!" snorted Thomas. "We'll show them."

"And Percy here will help, too," said Sir Topham Hatt.

"Oh, Sir! Yes, Sir! Please, Sir!" answered Percy excitedly.

Edward and Thomas worked the line. Starting at opposite ends, they pulled the trains, whistling cheerfully to each other as they passed.

Percy sometimes puffed along the branch line. Thomas was anxious, but both Driver and Guard promised to take care of Annie and Clarabel.

There were fewer trains, but the passengers didn't mind; they knew the three other engines were having a Lesson.

Henry, Gordon and James stayed shut in the shed, and were cold, lonely and miserable. They wished now they hadn't been so silly.

Now flip the book over to start another Thomas & Friends adventure.

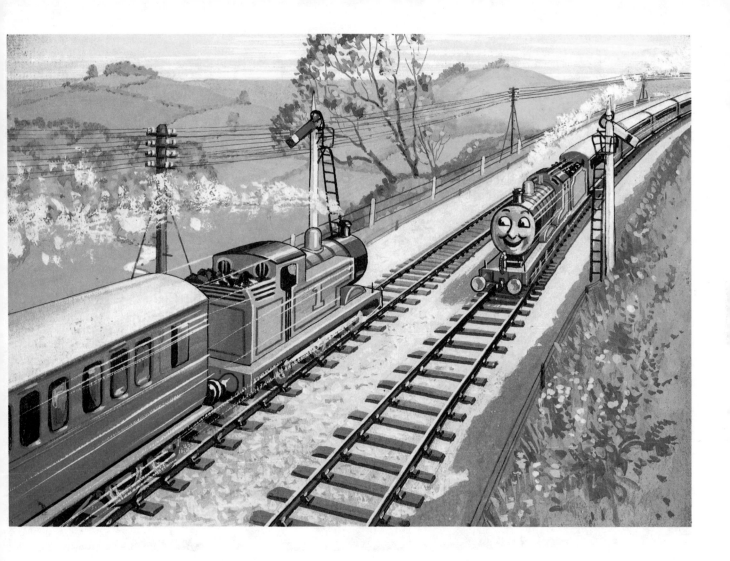

That night Henry, Gordon and James had an "indignation meeting."

"It's shameful to treat Tender Engines like this! Henry gets 'hooshed' by elephants; Gordon has to go backward and people think he's a Tank Engine. James spins around like a top, and everyone laughs at us. And added to that, Sir Topham Hatt makes us shunt in dirty sidings. Ugh!!" said all three engines together.

"Listen," said Gordon. He whispered something to the others. "We'll do it tomorrow. Sir Topham Hatt *will* look silly!"

14

Now flip the book over to start another Thomas & Friends adventure.

"I mustn't stick," thought James anxiously, as he ran to the turntable later. He stopped on just the right place to balance the table. It could now swing easily. His Fireman turned the handle . . . James turned . . . much too easily! The wind puffed him round like a top. He couldn't stop . . . !

At last the wind died down, and James stopped turning, but not before Gordon, who had been turned on the loop line, had seen him.

"Well! Well!" he said, "are you playing roundabouts?"

Poor James, feeling quite giddy, rolled off to the shed without a word.

Gordon came to the platform. Some little boys shouted, "Come on quick, here's a new Tank Engine."

"What a swiz!" they said, when they came near, "it's only Gordon, back to front."

Gordon hissed emotionally.

He puffed to the junction. "Hullo!" called Thomas, "playing Tank Engines? Sensible engine! Take my advice, scrap your tender and have a nice bunker instead."

Gordon snorted, but didn't answer. Even James laughed when he saw him. "Take care," hissed Gordon, "you might stick, too."

"No fear," chuckled James, "I'm not so fat as you."

His Driver tried to make him stop in the right place; backward and forward they went, but Gordon wasn't trying.

At last Gordon's Driver gave it up. The Fireman tried to turn the handle, but Gordon's weight and the strong wind prevented him. The Driver, some Platelayers, and the Fireman all tried together.

"It's no good," they said at last, mopping their faces, "your tender upsets the balance. If you were a nice Tank Engine, you'd be all right. Now you'll have to pull the next train backward."

Arrived at the Terminus, Gordon waited till all the passengers got out; then, groaning and grumbling, he shunted the coaches to another platform.

"Disgraceful! Disgraceful!" he hissed as he ran backward to the turntable.

The turntable was in a windy place close to the sea. It was only just big enough for Gordon, and if he was not on it just right, he put it out of balance, and made it difficult to turn.

Today, Gordon was in a bad temper, and the wind was blowing fiercely.

"You don't understand, little Thomas," said Gordon, "we Tender Engines have a position to keep up. You haven't a Tender and that makes a difference. It doesn't matter where *you* go, but We are Important, and for Sir Topham Hatt to make us shunt freight cars, fetch coaches, and go on some of those dirty sidings it's—it's—well it's not the Proper Thing."

And Gordon puffed away in a dignified manner.

Thomas chuckled and went off with Annie and Clarabel.

The big stations at both ends of the line each have a turntable. Sir Topham Hatt had them made so that Edward, Henry, Gordon and James can be turned around. It is dangerous for Tender Engines to go fast backward. Tank Engines like Thomas don't need turntables; they can go just as well backward as forward.

But if you had heard Gordon talking a short while ago, you would have thought that Sir Topham Hatt had given him a tender just to show how important he was.

Tenders and Turntables

by
The REV. W. AWDRY

SCHOLASTIC INC.

New York   Toronto   London   Auckland   Sydney
Mexico City   New Delhi   Hong Kong   Buenos Aires

Thomas the Tank Engine & Friends

A BRITT ALLCROFT COMPANY PRODUCTION

Based on The Railway Series by The Rev W Awdry
© Gullane (Thomas) LLC 2002

Visit the Thomas & Friends web site at www.thomasthetankengine.com

ISBN 0-439-33849-2

12 11 10 9 8 7 6 5 4 3 2 1   2 3 4 5 6 7/0
Printed in the U.S.A.
First Scholastic printing, May 2002

This edition is available for distribution only through the direct-to-home market.